The Big Ideas Club Presents

Living Myths

Revisiting Ancient Greece

The Hero's Madness

Two Tragedies: Herakles and Washington

By Jason Kassel, PhD

© 2025

Recursive Publishing

Euripides' Madness 2
Washington's Madness 61

Herakles' Madness

Episode 01: Introduction to Amphitryon

Scene: A bare and desolate courtyard. An old man stands in front of a glass container with the Constitution inside. Two small boys huddle around a woman who holds an infant. Three old men walk onto the stage.

Chorus1: Hey, look!

Chorus2: Yeah?

Chorus1: It's Amphitryon! He's about to speak.

Chorus2: I know him.

Chorus1: Everyone knows Amphitryon! He is the mortal man who raised Hercules.

Chorus2: Yes, everyone always says Amphitryon, father of Hercules.

Chorus1: That's because he's the mortal father who raised Hercules.

Chorus2:　But everyone knows that Hercules' true father is Zeus!

Chorus1:　That's why we always say Hercules, son of Zeus.

Chorus2:　Hercules was raised by the mortal man Amphitryon but born from Zeus.

Chorus3:　Shh! I want to listen to what he has to say.

Amphitryon:　Everyone knows me.　I am Amphitryon of Argos.　I raised Hercules, the half-immortal who was born from Zeus.　I stand here to say that Hercules has left his wife and sons unprotected while he traveled to Argos, our family's homeland.

Chorus1:　Oh, no!　Hercules has left his family alone!

Chorus2:　Why would a father leave his family?

Chorus3:　Shhh!

Amphitryon:　Hercules should be ruling Argos, but he can't live there because I was exiled.　I raised my family in Thebes and Hercules has to raise his family here as well.

Chorus1:   It wasn't Amphitryon's fault his uncle died.

Chorus2:   No, it was a complete accident but he was still exiled.

Amphitryon: Hercules went to Argos to ask the King, who happens to be his cousin, for permission to return so that he can raise his family in his homeland.

Chorus1:   Can you imagine Hercules having to ask permission?

Chorus2:   Hercules is so close to Zeus why should he ever need permission?

Amphitryon: The King and Hercules made a deal. Hercules can return to Argos with his family, but only if he civilizes the earth and frees the world of savage monsters.

Chorus1:   All that he has to do is civilize the earth? But that is impossible!

Chorus2:   How can a single human being civilize the entire earth?   It took generations just to civilize Greece!

Chorus3:   This request is too much.   Hercules will never be able to civilize the earth! Who came up with such a preposterous idea?

Amphitryon: I think this idea to civilize the earth was hatched by Hera but it may be Hercules' fate.

Chorus3: Hera!   She hates Hercules. Amphitryon, where is your son now?

Amphitryon: Last time anyone saw Hercules, he had begun his last labor. He was on his way down into Hades, the land where dead people live. Part of his promise to civilize the earth involves bringing Cerberus, the three-headed dog that guards the exit so dead people don't leave up to the surface.

Chorus1:   Wait a second! Are you telling me Hercules has gone to Hades? But that is where the dead live. No living person can go to Hades and come out alive.

Chorus2:   Does Hercules think he isn't mortal?

Chorus3:   If you go to the place where the dead live then you must stay dead.

Chorus1:   What is going to happen to Hercules' wife and sons now that he is in the land where the dead live? No one has ever returned from that place alive.

End Episode 01

Episode 2: Introduction to Chorus

Chorus1:   Oh, I wish I could help!

Chorus1:   Yes, but how? We are old!

Chorus1:   Look at me! I walk hunched over and use a walking stick.

Chorus1:   I sing sad songs and lament my old age.

Chorus1:   This is our swan song.

Chorus1:   We are nothing.

Chorus1:   We are so old.

Chorus1:   Oh, I am just a voice.

Chorus1:   I am a ghost.

Chorus1:   Like a dark vision from sleep.

Chorus1:   Oh, look at me! I am old and palsied with ancient legs.

Chorus1:   I wish I could help Amphitryon but I can't.

Chorus1:   None of us can.

Chorus1:   Oh, we are too old!

Chorus1:   Look at Hercules' three sons.

Chorus1:   The poor children have no father.

Chorus1:   Oh, why can't we be young again? Why can't we carry spears and win wars for Greece?

Chorus1:   Remember our youth?

Chorus1:   It was so wonderful to be young and strong.

Chorus1:   Look at Hercules' sons!

Chorus1:   Their eyes.

Chorus1:   They flash like their father's.

Chorus1:   Oh, if these boys die, how many allies will Greece lose?

End Episode 02

Episode 3: Introduction to Lykos

Chorus1: Here comes the evil tyrant.

Chorus1: He is a foreigner. Let's not use his real name. Let's call him Wolf. He came to our land without anyone's permission and took over.

Chorus3: He is like a wolf. We were nice to him and then he killed King Creon. He is a bad leader.

Chorus1: He brought sickness to our land.

Chorus2: Because of him, the political situation is bad. Everyone is fighting and no one can make decisions.

Chorus3: Shhh! I want to hear what he's saying to Amphi.

Lykos: Hey, Amphitryon and Megara. Yes, you two. I have a question for you and you must answer me. I am your king, after all.

Chorus1: Listen to that tone!

Chorus2: The tyrant shouldn't speak to Amphi like that.

Chorus3: Shhh! I want to listen.

Lykos: Aren't the two of you ready to die? Seriously, how much longer do you want to embarrass yourselves by staying alive? Hercules isn't returning from Hades. No one comes back from Hades. Plus, listening to the two of you moan and groan about death is too ridiculous. Amphi, don't you want to die and say hello to the god Zeus who slept with your wife and is Hercules' true father? And you, Meg, you are a woman who brags and boasts to everyone about the great hero you're married to. the greatest hero on earth. cuckolded your wife. You tell everyone you're married to the greatest hero on earth. Why? Because he killed a snake on the marshed? Or a lion from Nemea? Your son took advantage of a story. He caught it in a snare and told everyone he caught it with his bare hands. You think this is the man who will save you from your death? Are these the excuses for waiting before your sons are put to death? Hercules may have been a courageous hunter but not a warrior. He is a coward who has never strapped a shield to his arm or gone eye-to-eye with a man holding a spear. He uses a bow! A coward's weapon. What courage does it take to use a bow? Courage comes from using a spear and standing your ground. That's courage! That's bravery! Old man, don't think I'm cruel. I know I sit on the throne because I killed Megara's father Creon. If I allow these boys to grow, they will seek revenge.

Amphitryon (eyes to the heavens)

Hercules, listen to my words. I understand your birth. I shall show how ignorant this man is about you. I won't allow him to insult my son! First, my son, the most despicable slander - cowardice - has been made. Let the gods be my witness as I speak against this despicable slander.

Ask Pholoe if he thinks Zeus was a coward when he shot the earth-sprouted giants? Ask the wild, four-legged centaurs who they think is the bravest of all men. They will speak of my son, the one you call a pretend hero?

If you still don't believe in Hercules' bravery then go to Euboa - where you're from - and ask about your name. Will they sing your praises? What will they praise? What brave deed have you executed in your own country?

Keep insulting the bow and arrow - the cleverest of inventions - the archer's weapon. Listen closely to what I'm about to say. On the battlefield, a soldier is a slave to weight of his weapons and to his fellow soldiers. If a soldier lacks courage and runs, his battle-mates die - not through their cowardice but through someone else's. .

And what if the soldier's spear breaks and he has no other weapon? The archer, after having shot countless arrows, still has more to help avert death. The wisest tactic in battle is to kill the enemy and not allow him to kill you. An archer stands back, where the enemy can't see him, and he shoots arrows they can't see. He wounds, kills, and repels with no danger to himself, since he is hidden from their view.

You call my son a coward but you are frightened of his children! Logic says it is you who are the coward and I find it hard to accept how Zeus could do this to us. We are better than you. We should be delivering this fate to you.

Still, if you are determined to steal the throne, let us leave. Send us into exile. Avoid violence. Be careful the winds of fortune don't veer round and send violence in your direction.

Everyone who lives in the land of Cadmus. I accuse you! You have failed Hercules' sons. The man who faced the Minyan army and saved Thebes.

How can I praise Greece or stay silent about how this country has betrayed my son? Look at his sons. Every family in Greece should have provided protection of fire, spears, and shields. Where is their payment? Their father, my son, toiled and cleaned this country's land and ocean. Why won't Thebes or Greece protect them?

Poor boys! You see me as a weak old man who loves you but has nothing more than a noisy tongue. If you had only seen me in my youth. What vigor, what strength I had. My knees were once so strong and now age makes them quake. I was so strong but now I am weak with age. If I was young and strong I would grab a spear and soak this man in his own red blood. I would watch him flee beyond the pillars of Atlas in cowardice.

End Episode 03

Introduction to Megara (Lines 275-311)

Megara: Old man, thank you for your words. Your virtuous indignation and anger at the injustice we suffer is welcome but please be careful. I don't want you to vent your anger and then have this tyrant punish you. Listen to me, Amphitryon and tell me whether you think I make sense. How can I risk my children's lives - lives I labored to bring forth - when fate has decided it is time to die? Yes, death is a dreadful fate. But why should we provide food for our enemy's pleasure? They will torture us with fire and laugh while they watch us burn. The thought of that shame is worse than death. We must act with virtue while standing in the palace of Zeus. Amphitryon, how can you act like a coward after being so heroic and glorious on the battlefield. Do you desire a coward's death? My husband's reputation is as a brave and virtuous man. If his children die a coward's death they will carry the stain of cowardice. That would afflict their parents with disgrace. I must act the same way because a wife's actions must match her husband's. Hercules wouldn't choose a coward's death and neither will I. Amphitryon, I have weighed your hope. Hercules will not return from the world of the dead below the earth. No one has ever returned from Hades' halls. And, do you think this tyrant will soften because of words? Friendly overtures will not work on him. He is too stupid to make concessions or yield in any way. Only the wise and noble - men of breeding and wisdom - have a sense of decency and mercy. I had thought of exile. But to die in a foreign land? Our host's faces would look sweetly at banished friends and smile for a single day. Then we will die in abject poverty. A fate as miserable as death. Our family will be brave, Amphitryon. We are prepared for death whether we like it or not - it is our lot. Old man, bravery courses through your veins - it is in your blood. Struggling against the god, trying to escape your destiny, shows you have a fighting spirit but it is also strikingly foolish. Fate has decided and no one is able to alter the events that must take place.

End Episode 04

Megara Prepares for Death (Line 451-496)

Megara: Bring the priest to sacrifice, or butcher, these poor children. Come. We are ready to descend to Hades' halls. Who will murder me? We sacrificial victims are ready to be taken to Hades' halls. A mother, her children, and an old man. What an odd parade of the living dead. A shocking fate for me and a shocking fate for my children. Let my eyes fall on you one last time. I gave birth to you yet I have to watch my enemies insult, torment, then kill you - all for their own enjoyment. Hercules had given me so many words of hope. Those words have betrayed me. (Addressing each individually) Hercules was going to have you sit on the throne in Argos and wear his great lion skin armor over your head while ruling the great fertile land of the Pelasgians. Hercules was going to make you the ruler of Thebes - land of chariots - and place a carved wooden club in your right hand to defend against evil. Hercules was going to hand you Oechalia the country he conquered with his far-

shooting arrows.   Hercules, proud of his sons'
manliness, had three thrones chosen to exalt each of
you.   I was already choosing the best brides and
scheming to make Athens, Thebes, and Sparta allies
through marriage. This would have anchored your
life's cables and held your sheet-anchor steady. That
is gone now. The winds of your fortune have veered
and turned. Your brides are the spirits of death and
they have robbed me of my rights to give you your
bridal bath.   They only give me tears.   Your
grandfather is celebrating your marriage-feast and
accepted Hades as the father of your brides. I don't
know which of my sons to press to my bosom, which
to kiss first, and which to kiss last. What am I to do?
Which should I cling to? I wish I were a bee with
golden wings. I'd collect every sigh, blend them
together, and shed one copious tear. Hercules - Hear
my mortal words in the halls of Hades. Your father,
your sons, and your wife are dying and doomed. I was

once called blessed for marrying you. Come save me. Rescue your family. Even if you only come as a shadow. Your phantom presence would be enough to stop these child-killing cowards.

End Episode 05

Amphitryon Prepares for Death (Lines 497-513)

Amphitryon: Megara - prepare the funeral rites. I will raise my hands to the heavens in prayer to Zeus. I call on you to help these children - do you intend to help these children? I have prayed and invoked your name my entire life. Will you send aid or be unavailing and force death upon us? My life's toil has been wasted and my death is inevitable. (Turning to chorus) My old and aged friends. Life is too short and the joys of life are few. Live as best you can. Take heed. Pass through your days and nights as gladly as you may. Free of sadness and without a thought of sorrow through all time from morning till night. Old friends, time does not care about our hopes. He wrecks the little hope. Time flies and passes. Look at me. I am a man who made a mark amongst his fellows and achieved great fame. Among the mortals, I was known for doing great deeds. Fortune in a single day has robbed me of fame. I am like a feather that has been lifted up by wind and floats away toward the sky. Wealth, fame, high reputation - none of these are fixed or will stay with you always.

Farewell friends of my own age. Look upon your friend for this is the time I shall be seen.

End Episode 06

Episode 7

Introduction to Hercules

(Lines 523-561)

Hercules: Hello, Hercules has arrived home! I say hello to my house, hello to my doors, and hello to my household hearth. I feel such joy and happiness! I have emerged into the light! What is this sight that greets me? Why are my sons wearing outfits for funerals? Why is my wife standing among these old men? Why is my father weeping? Oh, has something bad happened while I was gone? Have I been struck by fate? Here comes my wife. I will find out.

Megara: Dearest of all mankind to me!

Amphitryon: You are a ray of light that has appeared to rescue your father! Is it really you? You have arrived just in time.

Hercules: Father, I don't understand. I arrived home to find confusion.

Megara: We are ruined and about to be killed. Forgive me, old friend, if I snatched words out of your mouth. You have more right to say the words than I. It is a woman's nature to speak in anguish and my children and I were being led to death.

Hercules: Oh, Apollo! What a sad prelude to your story.

Megara: Hercules, my brothers and father - Creon - are all dead.

Hercules: What befell him? Who dealt the fatal blow?

Megara: Lykos - our new splendid monarch - killed him.

Hercules: How? In a fair fight or battle? Was the country suffering from affliction? Was the land sick and weak?

Megara: Yes, sick with faction and civil war. Now he rules and is the master of Cadmus' city of seven gates.

Hercules: When I arrived, why were you terrified and panicked?

Megara: He was going to kill your father, me, and our sons.

Hercules: He feared my orphan babies?

Megara: He was afraid they would avenge Creon's death.

Hercules: They're dressed as though they're heading to their own funeral.

Megara: They're the garbs of the dead. For their funeral.

Hercules: You were all going to die a violent terrible death.

Megara: Hercules - We have been deserted by every friend and told you were dead.

Hercules: What put such a bleak and desperate thought in your heads?

Megara: Eurystheus' heralds and messengers proclaimed.

Hercules: Why do you abandon my home and hearth?

Megara: We were forced. They tossed and dragged your father from his bed.

Hercules: No mercy or shame to treat an old man so poorly?.

Megara: Mercy or shame? Lykos doesn't know the goddess.

Hercules: Was I so poor in friends? Were they rare in my absence?

Megara: Who has friends during a time of misfortune?

Hercules: They make light of, and forget, my warring with the Minyae?

Megara: Husband, I'll tell you again - Misfortune has no friends.

End Episode 07

Episode 8: Lykos Prepares to Kill Hercules' Family

Lines 701-725

Lykos: There you are. About time you came forth out of that palace, Amphitryon! Too much time, too long, putting on and arraying yourselves in the funeral clothes. Enough with the robes and trappings of the dead. Come, now, do as you've promised. Speak and tell Hercules' wife and sons to show themselves outside. Tell them to come out here and prepare to die on the conditions you yourselves offered.

Amphitryon: My king. Why do you persecute me for my misery? Your zeal is over and above the loss of my son, sir. You should be more moderate. You are my lord and master. Lord or not, I ask you to temper your zeal. Stop your insults while I grieve. But, yes, since you impose and press us to death's stern necessity, we acquiesce. We will do your will.

Lykos: Pray tell. Where is Megara? Where are the sons of Hercules?   Where are Alcmene's grandchildren?

Amphitryon: I believe, I guess, so far as I can make out, from outside, looking through this gate...

Lykos: Speak! What is she doing? What's going on? What do you see? Provide reasons not fancy.

Amphitryon: I see her sitting as a supplicant on the hallowed steps of Hestia's altar.

Lykos: Obviously. Praying uselessly and imploring to save her life.

Amphitryon: Yes, she's praying in vain. She's calling her dead husband back to life.

Lykos: A husband who is nowhere seen or will ever be seen. He is nowhere near, and will never come.

Amphitryon: Unless, perhaps, a god should resurrect him and raise him from the dead?

Lykos: Go to her inside the palace and bring her out here..

Amphitryon: If I do as you ask, I'll be complicit in her murder. Will you make me an accomplice?.

Lykos: Such a scruple bothers you. I have left fear behind and will bring out the mother and her children. Follow me, servants, no more delay. Time for our work of joy. Time to put a painless ending to this troublesome affair!

Amphitryon: Walk along the path. Go meet your fate. You perform evil deeds and others pay the price. Old and aged friends, Lykos enters the temple at precisely the right time. This murderer marches fairly to his doom.   He hopes to kill but will soon be entangled in a snare. Hercules' sword is waiting for him. This villain thinks he will slay his neighbors. I am going inside to watch him fall and die. The sight of a foe, an evil enemy, being slain and paying the full price for his deeds, gives pleasure. (Exit Amphitryon into the palace)

Chorus: Evil has changed sides and fortunes have turned.   Our once great mighty king has returned backward from the road to Hades. Hercules is alive! Hail justice and heavenly retribution.   The ever-turning will of the gods floods down.   This tyrant enters the palace of his death. He will be punished by death for the insolence shown against his betters. Joy floods my eyes and makes tears burst forth. Hercules has returned. The true king of this land. A thing never once thought in my heart. Retribution has been beyond my hopes and expectations.

End Episode 08

Episode 9: Lyssa and Madness Appear

(Lines 815-857)

Chorus: Old friends! An ominous apparition has descended and created a wild panic. What phantom fell and hovers over the palace? The same old fear and panic? Run! Run away friends! Rush your tardy feet and run! Lord Apollo! Lord, save us from this terror! (The chorus rushes about as if to flee or hide until Iris addresses them)

Iris: Have courage, men. Don't be afraid. I am Iris, handmaiden of the gods, and this is Madness, daughter of Night. We have not come to harm your city. We are marshaling for war against the house of one single man - Hercules, the son of Zeus and Alcmene. Now that he has accomplished his labors, neither fate nor Zeus can protect him from Hera's harm. Hera wants to stain him with the guilt of shedding kindred blood. He will slay his own children and wear the brand of spilling his sons' blood. And I agree with her on this decision. Come, unmarried virgin, daughter of black Night, harden your ruthless heart. Be relentless. Send your child-murdering frenzy forth upon Hercules. Stir up and confound his mind. Make his feet twitch and shudder. Goad him wildly on his mad career. Wind him up, shake out his sails, and set his sails of death up high. His own murderous hand will send his precious sons to Acheron's ferry in the world below. He will kill his children and then he will understand fiercely against him the raging anger Hera burns against him. If this man escapes punishment, the gods will become nothing,and the mortals' power will become everything.

Lyssa (MADNESS): I have a noble birth. Daughter of Night and sprung from Ouranos' blood. This birth grants me honors and prerogatives. I don't get any joy out of visiting the homes of men, and I don't use my power in anger against friends. Before I begin, Iris, I wish to counsel Hera and offer some advice before a grave error is made. If you will accept them, please hear my words. Both gods and mortals hold Hercules in high regard. He tamed the impassable land and the wild seas. On his own, with his mighty hand, he restored honor to the gods when godless men were destroying it with impiety. I personally counsel that, if it were me, I would rather be his friend than his enemy. I advise you not to plot evil against him and do not wish him dire mishaps.

Iris: Spare both Hera and I your advice. It is not needed..

Lyssa: I am trying to turn your steps. I want you to see the right way, not the wrong way. The best path instead of into one of evil.

Iris: Zeus' wife did not send you here to talk of self-control or wisdom.

End Episode 09

Epispde 10: Hercules Murders His Family

(Lines 922-1015)

Messenger: After Hercules killed the tyrant king, he threw his corpse outside the palace's halls. Around Zeus' altar stood sacrificial victims to purify the palace. His group of children, his wife Megara, and his old father stood around the altar like a lovely chorus. The holy basket of offerings was passed in a holy circle around the altar and we reverentially remained silent. Hercules began to dip the torch in his right hand into the holy water. He stopped, without a word, and stood in dumb-founded silence. His sons looked at him wondering why their father took so long. Hercules' face had changed. He looked distressed. His eyeballs were bloodshot and rolled wildly in their sockets. His bearded cheek oozed and was covered with foam. Eventually he spoke in a frenzied way and laughed a madman's laugh.

Hercules spoke. "Father, I won't perform this sacrifice unil I have also killed Eurystheus. Why kindle a flame and perform a purification ritual twice? I do not need to toil twice. With one stroke, in a single move, I will fix both problems. I will kill Eurystheus and bring his head here. I will cleanse and purify my hands of those I've already killed. Spill the water, throw it away. Rid your hands of the baskets. Somebody pass me my bow and arrows, and my club. I will travel to Mycenae with crowbars and pickaxes. I will tear down the iron foundations those Cyclope built with mason's hammers and Phoenician. I will heave them from their foundations with the city-walls. In his mind he headed to a chariot that didn't exist. He mounted a seat that didn't exist. He struck and goaded nonexistent horses with a nonexistent whip he held in his fingers. A twofold feeling filled the breasts of those around the altar. Half-amusement and half-fear, no one knew whether to laugh or cry. One looked at another. They wondered if Hercules had gone mad or if he was joking and making sport. Then Hercules began running around from one room in the palace to another. He finally stopped in the center of the men's quarters and announced that he had arrived at the city of Nisus. He threw himself and fell on the floor as though it were a feast table. He waited a bit, then began marching around the house. He said he had arrived near the plains amid the wooded valleys of the Isthmus. Thinking he was taking part in the Isthmus games, Hercules stripped naked and began wrestling a nonexistent opponent. He was both competitors and the herald. He proclaimed himself victor and called on nonexistent spectators to be silent and listen. Then his sick mind made him fancy he was in Mycenae. He shouted terrible and fearful threats against Eurystheus. His father grabbed his son's stalwart and sturdy arm. He addressed him. "My son, what is wrong? What do you mean by this strange behavior? Is your mind affected by the blood you've spilled? Has the blood of your victims driven you frantic?" In his mind, Hercules thought his father's hand was that of Eurystheus' father. Hercules saw his father as Eurystheus' father. He heard Eurystheus' father's voice, not his own father's, begging him not to kill his grandchildren. He thrust aside the hand he believed belonged to Eurystheus, brought arrows to his bow, and made ready his quiver. He was ready to slay Eurystheus' sons. His poor, frightened boys rushed and darted about. One clung to his hapless mother's garments. Another hid behind the shadow of a column. The third child cowered beneath the altar like a little bird. Their mother cried out and screamed at Hercules. "What are you doing? You are their father? Why do you want to kill your own children?" His old father and all the servants also yelled at him but he ran around the column hunting the child. Such dreadful circles. When he stood face to face with his son, he shot him through the heart. The boy fell on his back. Blood first sprinkled then splashed on the stone pillars. He gasped his last breath of life. Hercules saw his son fall and he gave a loud shout of triumph and joy. He boasted loudly, "Here lies one of Eurystheus' sons dead at my feet. Atoning for his father's hatred towards me." Hercules turned toward his second son, crouching at the altar's base hoping to escape the slaughter, and aimed his bow. Before he could fire, the boy threw himself at his father's knews. He flung his hand up to reach his father's beard or neck. "Do not slay me, father. Please do not kill me. I am your child. I am your son. I am no son of Eurystheus. You are not going to kill his sons. Hercules had the savage Gorgon-scowl. He turned his wild, monstrous gaze at his son, who was too close for his bow and arrow. Hercules raised his club above his head and, like a blacksmith, hammered his boy's blond head, and smashed his skull. After killing his second boy, he hunted for his third victim. The boy's mother quickly grabbed him, ran off inside the rooms, and shut all the doors behind her. Hercules believed he was in front of the Cyclops wall, and dug under the door using crowbars to lever them open. When the door posts fell, Hercules killed both his wife and son with a single shaft from his bow. Hercules ran off to look for his old father, but a phantom - in the guise of the goddess Athena - appeared brandishing a sharp spear in her hand, and wearing a plumed helmet. She grabbed a stone and hurled it at Hercules' chest. This stayed his madness and his frenzied thirst for blood. It sent him plunging to sleep. He fell on the ground and hit his back on one of the fallen columns. We regained our courage, aided his father and bound Hercules in thick ropes with knotted cords. He is tied to the column so he won't do any more harm when he wakes. There the poor man sleeps. Not the best spot, the spot where he murdered his own children and wife. For my part, that man inside the palace is the most unfortunate and miserable mortal.

End Episode 10

Episode 11: Hercules Realizes What He Has Done

Lines 1136-1162

Hercules: Father, what's wrong? Why do you weep? Why do you stand so far from me? I am the son you love so dearly.

Amphitryon: Yes, you are my son. Even after all the misery, you are my son and child.

Hercules: Misery? What misery? Why are you crying?

Amphitryon:　Oh, my son! Even a god would weep and cry after suffering this misery.

Hercules: That is a bold and terrible thing to say! But, you still haven't told me what misery I am responsible for. You haven't explained what I've done.

Amphitryon:　My son, use your senses. Your own eyes see the misery. It is all around us.

Hercules: Father, no more riddles. Sketch the scene and explain.

Amphitryon:　I will explain once I'm sure your mind has recovered and you aren't mad as a fiend of hell.

Hercules: Tell me! What new life disasters do these dark suspicious hints represent?

Amphitryon:　I will but I don't know if you have sober senses or still remain in the grips of Hades' madness.

Hercules: I don't remember being mad!

Amphitryon: Old friends, shall I loosen and undo my son's ropes? Tell me, what should I do?

Hercules: Yes, loosen and undo my ropes. Say the name of who bound and tied me. I feel shame to be treated this way.

Amphitryon: This shame is enough. Rest content. You don't need to know about your troubles. Forget the rest.

Hercules: Enough of this. My silence won't provide the answer? Tell me what happened to me.

Amphitryon: Oh Zeus, in your throne up there seated next to Hera, can you see these deeds proceeding?

Hercules: Hera! Have I suffered from her enmity? Hera attacked me?

Amphitryon: Come now, a truce with the goddess. Leave her alone. Take care of your own troubles.

Hercules: I am undone. I am destroyed. A disaster will unfold I must endure.

Amphitryon: My son, look at the bodies. See your children's corpses.

Hercules: Or horror! What hideous sight is here? What sorrow is this?

Amphitryon: My son, against your sons you waged an unnatural war.

Hercules: War? What do you mean? Say who killed these children.

Amphitryon: You and your arrows, my son. And a god brought it all about.

Hercules: Father, what are you saying? What have I done? Speak as the messenger of evil news.

Amphitryon: I am saying, my son, you went distraught and, in a fit of madness, killed your sons. Your questions receive sad answers.

Hercules: Have I also murdered my wife?

Amphitryon: Yes. All this, Hercules, is the work of your own unaided hand.

Hercules: Woe is me. I'm wrapped in a cloud of sorrow and surrounded by sighs and groans.

Amphitryon: I lament and groan for the fate you suffer, my son

Hercules: Did I smash this palace to pieces or incite others?

Amphitryon: I only know that your life is undone and you are ruined.

Hercules: Where was I when my frenzied madness seized me and destroyed my life?

Amphitryon: In the moment it seized you, you were standing by the altar, and purifying your hands with the fire.

Hercules: Why did I not murder myself? Why murder my darling sons and spare my own life? Should I not go and leap or hurl myself off some sheer cliff? Should I dig my sword into my entrails? Should I aim the sword against my heart to bring justice and avenge my children's blood? Should I throw my flesh onto a pyre? Burn my body in the fire to escape the life of hatred and infamy that now awaits me? Before I practice my plans to die, I have a new hurdle to jump. Theseus, my friend and relative, is coming. The eyes of my dearest friend will become polluted if he sees me as a murderer of own children. What can I do now? Where can I find release from my sorrow and escape this grief? Should I take wings and soar to the heavens or sink and plunge down beneath the earth? I'll veil my head in the darkness of my cloak. I am ashamed. The shame of the blood-guiltiness I have done to my children is too great. If I were to let an innocent man's eyes fall on me, the innocent could be harmed for my sin of spilling blood.

End Episode 11

Lesson 12: Introduction to Theseus

Lines 1198-1228

Theseus: Old friend, I have arrived with young Athenian warriors. Armed and encamped, we are waiting by Asopos' streams of Asopos. We have arrived to help Hercules, your son. The city received a rumor from Erecheis that Lykos usurped this city, became your enemy, and waged war against you. When I heard this, I came to make recompense for his kind deed and see if Hercules needs any help. He saved me from the underworld. If needed, I and my allies are here to provide aid.But what is this heap of dead? The ground is already covered in corpses. Am I too late? Did a delay fail to stop new disasters? Who murdered these children? Whose wife is this here? Boys are not sent to battle or war. I must be discovering another type of disaster.

Amphitryon: Lord Theseus, from the land of olive trees!

Theseus: Such a sad and piteous greeting Amphitryon!

Amphitryon: The heavens have delivered and afflicted us great suffering, lord!

Theseus: Whose children are these that you are weeping and grieving?

Amphitryon: My own son's children, Theseus. My unfortunate son. He was their father and butcher both. His heart hardened when he did the bloody deed.

Theseus: What? What are you saying, Amphitryon? How did this happen?

Amphitryon: In a wild fit of frenzied madness, he shot arrows dipped in the hundred-headed Hydra's blood..

Theseus: Stop, Amphitryon. Use good words.

Amphitryon: Oh, how I wish I could do that, Theseus!

Theseus: What dreadful things you say!

Amphitryon: Fortune has spread her wings, and we are ruined. We are gone! This is our end!

Theseus: I see Hera's work and carnage. Who is this man lying here among the corpses, old man?

Amphitryon: My son, the enduring warrior. A son of many miseries who marched with gods on the plains of Phlegra where they fought together and killed the giants.

Theseus: Woe for him. Was a mortal's fortune ever as cursed or caused a man to suffer so much?

Amphitryon: Never will you find another mortal who has borne a larger share of suffering, been more fatally deceived, or who has been so tortured as he.

Theseus: Why does he veil his head with his cloak?

Amphitryon: Your kind intent makes him ashamed to meet your eyes. The shame of facing you after murdering his sons is too great..

Theseus: Uncover his head.   I have come to sympathize and share in his grief.

Amphitryon: Son, pull away that cover from your eyes. Let the sun see your face. It is a hard task to stand up against one's tears. (He kneels beside

Hercules) My son, my aged eyes shed tears as I grasp your beard, your knees, and by your hands. My child, restrain your savage lion's temper. You are rushing forth across a path of unholy bloodshed, eager to add one woe upon another.

End Episode 12

Lesson 13: Hercules Contemplates Suicide

Lines 1239-1253

Theseus (To Hercules): Hey, you. Yes, you. Lying down there, huddled in the depths of your misery. I am calling you. Come and show your face to your friends. The darkest blackness wouldn't hide the pains of this catastrophe. (Hercules motions him to look at the corpses and to go away) I don't speak in hand gestures. Are you trying to say something about murder? Are you afraid to pollute me with your words? It doesn't matter to me, Hercules. So what if I suffer and share your fate. Whatever good fortune I have, started when you brought me safely from the dead to the light of life. I hate a friend whose gratitude grows old. It is a terrible man who sails in a friend's happy moments but is unwilling to share the ship of poor fortune with him. Arise, Hercules, and uncover your poor face. Look at me, you poor wretch. The noble gallant soul accepts and endures, without a word, the death blows sent by the gods.

Hercules: Like no other man, I am afflicted with suffering misfortunes.

Theseus: Hercules, your misfortunes stretch from the earth to the heavens.

Hercules: And that's why I've resolved to prepare myself to die.

Theseus: How would that help? Do you think the gods care about such threats?

Hercules: The heavens have been remorseless and the gods arrogant. I shall act in kind.

Theseus: Hold your tongue, Hercules. Your presumptuous words could bring you even more pain and suffering.

Hercules: My ship is freighted with pains of sorrow. I have no room or space to stow anything more.

Theseus: So what are you going to do? Where is your fury drifting you? How far will your anger take you?

Hercules: I will die again and return to the world below from where I have come - the Underworld.

Theseus: Hercules, your words, language, and speech are the same as a common person.

Hercules: You speak without knowing my grief and your advice is outside sorrow's pale, Theseus.

Theseus: Are these the words of the much-endured mighty Hercules?

Hercules: I have endured but this is too much. Endurance must come in moderation. Endurance must have a limit.

Theseus: I am speaking with Hercules, the mighty benefactor and ally of mortals?

Hercules: Mortals have never helped me. Hera has her way. She controls all this.

Theseus: Greece will never allow Hercules to die such a perverse and mindless death.

Hercules: Hear me and listen as I reason. I will list with words why my death will not be mindless. Listen as I unfold the reasons why my life now, and in the past, has been unbearable to me. Let me start with my birth. I was born to a father who had the stained guilt of bloodshed. Before he married my mother, he murdered his old father-in-law. When a race is born of badly laid foundations, all descendants are fated to live a cursed and miserable life.

Then Zeus - whoever this Zeus might be - begot me so I would be the focus of Hera's hatred. (Theseus visibly objects to this.) Don't be upset. I regard you as my true father and not Zeus. While still a breastfeeding baby, Hera sent fierce snakes into my cradle to kill me. After I grew to become a man, firm flesh covered my young body, I performed labor and toil. What is the point of talking about them all now? Why talk about the lions? The three-bodied Typhons? The giants? Forget about the battle against an army of four legged Centaurs. Forget the hydra, that beast with the many heads that kept growing back. I performed countless tasks before ending in the Underworld where I obeyed Eurystheus' command and brought the three-headed dog up to the light of the sun. (Indicating the corpses) This bloody deed is my last labor I perform. I crowned the sorrows and miseries of my house with my own sons' murder. I have arrived at this sorry state. I love Thebes but piety forbids me from living here. No longer may I dwell in the city I love. If I did stay, which temple or to what friends could I turn? No friendly greetings or invitations will follow the horror of my curse. I can't go to Argos because I'm an exile from my own country. Another city but which one? And even if one exists, I don't think I could endure the sneers, the painful jabs, the bitter tongues, all thrown at men with a bad name. I can hear them all say, "Oh look, that is Zeus' son who killed his wife and sons? Why doesn't he get the hell out of our land?" Theseus, for a man like me, who was always known for being blessed, such change is unbearable. For a man who always endured such a miserable life, a change would not bother him. Misery has always been a part of him. I think, Theseus my misfortune will deliver me to the point where the earth will roar out to me, "Do not touch my soil." The sea and the streams of all the rivers will say, "I forbid you from crossing them." I shall become like the first men who shed kin blood - the Ixion - who are chained to a spinning wheel in the Underworld for all eternity. I once shared a joyful fortune with the Greeks, it would be best that I never be seen by them. What is the good of living such a useless and damned life? Let gorgeous Hera blissfully dance in her divine slippers on top of Olympus' sparkling floors. Hera has achieved her goal and toppled the best of mortals right down to his foundations. What man would offer prayers to such a goddess? Her jealousy - born of her husband's visit to a mortal woman's bed - drives her to destroy an innocent man who has done humanity good.

End Episode 13

Episode 14: Theseus Provides Hercules with Reasons to Live

Theseus: You are correct that this is Hera's work but think carefully if this is your reason to die. Hercules, if I believed the gods cursed your life while providing every other mortal a life free of troubles then I would advise you to go ahead and die. But there's no mortal who hasn't been touched by misery. No god, either, if what the poets say is true. Gods have gone to each other's bed, committed sinful unions, and, to become king, they fettered their fathers with shameful chains. Yet they still continue on with their sinful lives on Mount Olympus. Are you a mortal who judges sins more harshly than the gods, who see no wrong at all in their sin. Obey the law, Hercules, leave Thebes, and come with me to Athens. I will cleanse your hands of all blemishes, give you a home, and a portion of my wealth. I will give you the gifts the Athenians gave when I saved seven boys and seven girls by killing the Knossos' Minotaur. They have given countryside plots of land and, while you live, people will know them as being yours. When you die and go to the Underworld, the whole of Athens will worship you as their hero with sacrifices and huge monuments. In the eyes of Greeks, Athens will be a garland of achievement. They will speak well of the city for performing a good deed to a hero such as Hercules. This is how I will repay you for saving my life. I see that you are in need of friends. When the gods honor us with good fortune, Hercules, we do not need friends. A god's help, if and when he chooses to give it, is enough.

End Episode 14

Episode 15: Hercules Chooses to Live

Hercules: Dear friend, these things you said about the gods are side issues and have nothing to do with my present troubles. In any case, I don't believe that the gods engage in such unholy relationships. I have never believed, and I won't believe now, the story about gods tying up their parents in chains. I don't believe one god is the lord of another because a real god doesn't need anything. Poets invent miserable tales. Though I'm still in misery, I have had a thought. If I kill myself, people might think I am a coward. If a man cannot stand against misfortune, how can he stand against an enemy's arrow? I'll hold on to life and come with you to your city. I thank you profusely. (Hercules wipes a tear from his eye) I have tasted pain and have rejected none. I have shed no tears nor did I think I ever would. But now it seems I must be Fate's slave. (To Amphitryon) Old father, I am now both murderer and exile. Give my sons a proper burial, father. The law forbids me to put their burial clothes back on and shed a tear in their honor. Let them lie against their mother's breast, in her arms, a communion of misery. Poor mother whom I unwittingly killed. After the burial, stay in this city, father. It will not be easy, but strengthen your heart to share in my misery. (Turning to the children)

My murdered sons. You have been deprived of your father's inheritance, the great fame of my glorious labor. It would have been bestowed upon you had you lived. And you, my poor wife, I killed you most unjustly. How unjustly I repaid you for your loyalty to our marriage bed and for watching over our household during my long absence. My poor wife, my poor sons, and poor me. (He bends over the bodies and kisses their foreheads) Sweet pitiful kisses. Should I keep my weapons or throw them away? If I wear them, they will dangle about my sides and call out, "We are the weapons you used to kill your wife and children. We are their murderers. Why are you still holding on to us?" How could I justify carrying them? Should I strip myself of these weapons? These weapons helped me perform glorious deeds throughout Greece. Should I get rid of my weapons and leave myself vulnerable to my enemies? I will die a death of shame. No, I must keep my weapons and their misery. Theseus, do me the favor of coming with me to Argos. There is a reward I earned for bringing back that savage dog, Cerberus. If you don't come with me, who knows what I might do on my own. My sadness for my sons might cause me to do some harm to myself. Thebes! All of you Thebans! Cut off your hair, join me in my mourning, attend the burial of my sons, and shed tears for all of us. We have all been destroyed by Hera's cruel blow.

End Episode 15

Episode 16: Hercules and Theseus Leave for Athens

Theseus: Hercules, my friend, it is time for you to stop crying. Come, let's leave for Athens.

Hercules: I can't! My limbs are frozen.

Theseus: I understand. Even powerful people like yourself are overpowered by misfortune.

Hercules: I wish I could turn into a rock, because a rock doesn't have any memories and then I wouldn't have to remember all of my troubles.

Theseus: Enough of this. Give your hand to a helping friend.

Hercules: Oh, Theseus! Take care not to touch me. I don't want you polluted with themurder blood that stains my clothes.

Theseus: Hercules, leave it be. I am not concerned

Hercules: Oh, Theseus! Now that I have lost my sons, I shall regard you as a son.

Theseus: Come, put your arm around my neck and I'll lead the way.

Hercules: A pair of friends, one of which is wretched in his misery. Old father, this is the sort of friendship a person ought to make. One that is reciprocal. Where a friend stands next to you no matter what you've done.

Amphitryon: Theseus comes from Athens which is a good and blessed land.

Hercules: Oh, Theseus! Turn me around so that I can see my sons once more.

Theseus: Do you think it will work like some soothing drug?

Hercules: I need to see them again. Oh father, I need to put my arms around you!

Amphitryon: Here I am with a loving embrace, my son. We both wish the same thing.

Theseus: Hercules, have you forgotten all the glorious and mighty deeds you've done?

Hercules: Why do you ask about my deeds? Of course I haven't forgotten. But those deeds didn't cause me grief.

Theseus: You are speaking with too much emotion. This is not the way to win praise. If people see you acting like this they will say you behave without nobility.

Hercules: You think I lack nobility? Those weren't your words a moment ago.

Theseus: Well, Hercules, this grief and emotion is not noble behavior. The Hercules of the olden days, the glorious Hercules, wouldn't be weeping and crying. He would be brave.

Hercules: Theseus, how did you behave when you were in the Underworld?

Theseus: Even worse than you are now. In fact, I acted worse than any man who has ever lived. There is no one who would say that I acted without courage.

Hercules: Then how can you judge me?

Theseus: Exactly! Let's go, the city of Athena awaits!

Hercules: Farewell, old father!

Amphitryon: And to you too, my son!

Hercules: Father, please bury my sons according to the rituals.

Amphitryon: I will, my son. But what about me? Who will bury me, my son?

Hercules: I will, father.

Amphitryon: You will? When?

Hercules: After your death, father.

Amphitryon: But how? You are going to be banished? I don't understand.

Hercules: Father, don't worry. I will bring you to Athens but you are burdened with burying my sons and living here alone in Thebes. And I, a person who has shamefully murdered his wife and sons, will follow Theseus like a small boat following a large one.

I say to everyone who will listen, good friends are better than wealth or power.

(All except the Chorus leave)

Chorus: Let us leave this place full of tears and sadness. We have lost our best friends.

Exit all

End of Madness "Hercules"

Washington's Madness

Episode 01: Introduction to George Washington

Scene: A courtyard in front of a house. An old man looks at a wall with a large painted U.S. Constitution. Two small boys huddle around a woman who holds an infant. Three old men walk onto the stage.

Chorus1: Hey, look!

Chorus2: Yeah?

Chorus1: It's Rambo! He's about to speak.

Chorus2: I know him.

Chorus1:   Everyone knows Rambo! He raised George Washington.

Chorus2:   Yes, everyone always says Rambo, father of George Washington.

Chorus1: Like I said, Rambo raised George Washington.

Chorus2: But everyone knows that George Washington's true father is American ideals!

Chorus1: That's why we always say George Washington, son of American ideals.

Chorus2:   George Washington was raised by Rambo but born from American ideals.

Chorus3:   Shh! I want to listen to what he has to say.

Rambo: Everyone knows me. I am Rambo and I raised George Washington who was born from American ideals. I stand here to say that George Washington has abandoned his family and left his wife and his sons without protection. George

Washington has chosen violence and adventure instead of his family.

Chorus1: Oh, no! George Washington has left his family alone!

Chorus2: Why would a father leave his family?

Chorus3: Shhh!

Rambo: While George Washington has been away, our city has become controlled by the foreign leader Putin Xi who plans to murder George Washington's family.

Chorus1: But why did George Washington leave his family alone?

Rambo: Because he can't help himself. He continually craves adventure and excitement. He is too angry and has been fighting for so long that he's forgotten how to live a peaceful life. He thinks if he fights, and fights, and fights his problems will all be solved.

Chorus1: That's too bad. George Washington shouldn't want to fight so much. He's too angry.

Rambo: Yes, I know. In his anger, he promised to round up all the mathematicians and scientists in order to create a time travel device.

Chorus1: George Washington has promised to create time-travel?

Rambo: That's right! I don't know if it was because his cousin goaded him or if it was John Lennon. But, for whatever reason, that's what he agreed to do.

Chorus1: George Washington can't solve time-travel! That's ridiculous.

Chorus2: How can George Washington solve time-travel? Think about all the brilliant minds that have tried.

Chorus3: This is too much! George Washington will never be able to create time-travel.

Chorus3:   John Lennon hates George Washington!
Oh George Washington, where is George Washington
now?

Rambo: Last time anyone saw him, he was on his
way to bring Andy Warhol to this time period. He
promised his cousin he'd travel back in time, find
Andy Warhol, and bring him to this time period.
George Washington said he's going to bring Andy
Warhol back and make everyone famous for fifteen
minutes.

Chorus1:   Wait a second! Are you telling me George
Washington has gone back in time?   But that is
impossible. Once he goes back in time, he'll change
everything and the present won't be the present
anymore.

Chorus3:   Oh, what a conundrum! Why did George
Washington have to make such a promise?

Chorus1:   What is going to happen to George
Washington's wife and sons? He has abandoned them

in anger and is now off in pursuit of Andy Warhol in order to make everyone famous for fifteen minutes. Because of his absence, his enemies are going to kill his family.

End Episode 01

Episode 02: Introduction to Chorus

Chorus1:   Oh, I wish I could help!

Chorus1:   Yes, but how? We are old!

Chorus1:   Look at me! I walk hunched over and use a walking stick.

Chorus1:   I sing sad songs and lament my old age.

Chorus1:   This is our swan song.

Chorus1:   We are nothing.

Chorus1:   We are so old.

Chorus1:   Oh, I am just a voice.

Chorus1:   I am a ghost.

Chorus1:   Like a dark vision from sleep.

Chorus1:   Oh, look at me! I am old and palsied with ancient legs.

Chorus1:   I wish I could help George Washington but I can't.

Chorus1:   None of us can.

Chorus1:   Oh, we are too old!

Chorus1:   Look at George Washington's three sons.

Chorus1:   The poor children have no father.

Chorus1:   Oh, why can't we be young again? Why can't we carry big guns and win wars anymore?

Chorus1:   Remember our youth?

Chorus1:   It was so wonderful to be young and strong.

Chorus1:   Look at George Washington's sons!

Chorus1:   Their eyes.

Chorus1:   They flash like their father's.

Chorus1:   Oh, if these boys die, how many allies will we lose?

End Episode 02

Episode 03: Introduction to Putin Xi

Chorus1:   Here comes Putin Xi.

Chorus1:   He is a bad leader.

Chorus1:   He brought sickness to our land.

Chorus2:   Because of him, our political situation has deteriorated and no one makes decisions.

Chorus3:   Shhh! I want to hear what Putin Xi and Rambo are saying to one another.

Putin Xi: Hey, Rambo and Betsy Ross. Yes, you two. I have one question for each of you and since I have taken over and control everything, you must answer all of my questions truthfully.

Chorus1:   Listen to that tone!

Chorus2:   Putin Xi shouldn't speak to Rambo like that.

Chorus3:   Shhh! I want to listen.

Putin Xi: Aren't the two of you ready to die? Seriously, how much longer do you want to embarrass yourselves by staying alive? George Washington isn't returning from time travel. No one returns from time travel. Plus, I think it is too funny listening to the two of you moan and groan about death. Rambo, all I ever hear is you talking about your son George Washington who was born to American ideals. And you, Betsy Ross, you keep saying George Washington is the best and most magnificent person ever. Why? Because someone said he crossed the Delaware on a boat?   Or he single-handedly created a country? Please give me a break!

Chorus1: Putin Xi shouldn't speak about George Washington like this!

Chorus2:   George Washington is a great general! The best, wisest, most clever general that ever lived.

Putin Xi: George Washington took advantage of people's gullibility. He spread rumors about sailing on a boat with soldiers when really they got their feet wet in the rain. This is certainly not the type of man who is capable of finding the scientists and mathematicians to create time travel and bring Andy Warhol here to make everyone famous for fifteen minutes! That's stupid and silly. George Washington may have been brave and strong once, but he is no true leader of men. He is a bad general, doesn't know how to issue commands, and no one ever respected him. George Washington got lucky in a few battles and then everyone latched onto some great myth.

Chorus1: Putin Xi lies! George Washington is brilliant. It was never luck, just sheer genius!

Chorus2: His command was perfect. People listened to his every word as if it came from the heavens.

Putin Xi: Look Rambo, between you and me, I don't want to kill George Washington's kids but I have to. You know the only reason I rule is because I killed Betsy Ross' father who had control. If I allow these boys to grow, they will seek revenge.

Rambo: You have said a lot of offensive things but I am going to focus on how you spoke about my son. First, you are a bad ruler who is a liar. George Washington never lost a battle in his life. He is a natural on the battlefield and commands men better than anyone who's ever lived. George Washington, my son, knows everything there is to know about war. He knows the guns, the formations, how to use technology, you name it and he knows how to do it. George Washington can do anything when it comes to war. He's already won wars that haven't been announced. He defeats enemies before they know what they confront. How dare you tell such lies about George Washington!

Chorus1:   Good for Rambo!

Chorus2:   It's about time someone stood up to Putin Xi!

Putin Xi: Rambo, for your tone I am going to kill you slowly. I am going to leave now but I will be back soon and when I do I am going to bring soldiers with me. We will put a huge bonfire together and roast your family alive.

Rambo: Everyone who lives in this land has abandoned George Washington's family.   George Washington saved everyone who lives here but none of them will step up and help.

Chorus1:   How can anyone think we are good or decent?   We aren't helping George Washington's family?

Chorus2:   We are too old to help.

Chorus1:   Well, where are the young people?   Why aren't the young people in this city helping Rambo protect   George   Washington's   family.   After everything George Washington has done, not a single young person is coming to help him.

Rambo: Oh, George Washington's poor sons! All I am to you is an old and weak man. I love you but I only have a mouth for words. If only I had the strength and vigor of my youth. I was so strong but now I am weak with age. If I was young and strong I would grab a weapon and soak Putin Xi in his own red blood or watch him run away in cowardice.

Chorus1:   Oh, we are too old and weak to help!

Chorus2:   Why have the young people in our city abandoned George Washington's family?

Chorus1:   What is going to happen to them now? Will the evil Putin Xi burn them alive?

End Episode 03

Episode 04: Introduction to Betsy Ross

Betsy Ross: Old men, I listen to your words and hear that you want to help. You can't do anything with your old and weak bodies but at least your words are soothing.

Chorus1:   Thank you.

Chorus1:   Thank you for understanding that we are too old and weak to help.

Chorus1:   We want to help.

Chorus1:   But we are powerless.

Betsy Ross: Rambo, my father-in-law, you must listen to me. I am no longer afraid of dying. Listening to that evil Putin Xi talk about my husband George Washington gave me courage and strength. Listen to what I have to say and tell me whether you think I make sense.

Chorus1:   What do you think Betsy Ross will say

Chorus1:   Strong women don't always say the same thing.   Sometimes different time periods define strength differently

Chorus1:   What do you mean?

Chorus1:   Well, let's hear what she says.

Betsy Ross: How can I risk my children's lives - lives I labored to bring forth - when fate has decided it is time to die? Yes, death is a dreadful fate. But why should we provide food for our enemy's pleasure? They will torture us with fire and laugh while they watch us burn. The thought of that shame is worse than death.

Chorus1: That sounds strong.

Chorus1: Yes. If she's going to die anyway, why should she let her enemies have the pleasure of seeing her suffer?

Betsy Ross: We must act with virtue. I won't die like a coward. I will face death with heroism as though I was on a battlefield. My husband's reputation is as a brave and virtuous man. If his children die a coward's death they will carry the stain of cowardice. I must act the same way because a wife's actions must match her husband's. George Washington wouldn't choose a coward's death and neither will I.

Chorus1: I don't like that so much.

Chorus1: That's what I was saying about different time periods and ideas of strength. For her, she is being strong by wanting to die to protect her husband's reputation.

Betsy Ross: Rambo, I have weighed your words. I do not believe George Washington will return from time travel with Andy Warhol to make everyone famous for fifteen minutes. No one has ever traveled through time.

Chorus1: She's pessimistic about her husband coming back.

Chorus2:   But she is being as brave as she can be.

Betsy Ross: Rambo, do you think Putin Xi will be kind to us if we beg and plead? Friendly overtures won't help our cause. Putin Xi has no sense of decency or mercy. I had thought of asking him to let us live by sending us into exile but it would be awful to die in a foreign land.   Our host's faces would smile for a single day and then they would let us die in abject poverty. A fate as miserable as death.

Chorus1:   She has no more hope. She has given up.

Chorus2:   But she faces death bravely. She stands tall like a warrior in the midst of a heated battle.

Betsy Ross: Rambo, our family will be brave and we are prepared for death. Struggling against destiny is foolish. Fate has decided we are to die and no one is able to alter the events that must take place.

End Episode 04

Episode 05: George Washington Prepares for Death

Chorus1:   I feel so badly for our friend Rambo and his son George Washington. I wish we could help him.

Chorus2:   Yes, so do I. But we are too old.

Chorus1:   We have no power.

Chorus2:   No one will listen to our reasons and we don't have the physical strength to force people to listen to our words.

Chorus1:   We used to command respect.

Chorus2:   Now, no one listens to the old and the young only think of themselves.

Chorus1:   Shhh! I want to hear our friend Rambo.

Rambo: Betsy Ross, if you believe it is your fate to die then you can prepare yourself for death. I have not given up hope that my son, George Washington, will return from his time travel with Andy Warhol who will make everyone famous for fifteen minutes.

Chorus1: Rambo hasn't given up hope!

Chorus2: He still has faith in the power of George Washington!

Rambo: There is nothing my son George Washington can't do! He was born from American ideals and as long as we continue to have faith in American ideals then George Washington will return. I place my hand on this copy of the Constitution and call on American ideals. Will you help protect these children? Will you help me after I have told everyone that American ideals gave birth to my son Rambo? I have always looked up to you and spoken of you with reverence. Now, when my enemies are near I ask American ideals to send aid? Please, avail yourself to us. Or, are you going to allow our enemies to burn us alive? Has my life's toil been wasted and is my death inevitable?

Chorus1:   Rambo's faith is being tested.

Chorus2:   He wants something in return for the faith he's given.

Chorus1:   No one is owed anything for their faith.

Chorus2:   But Rambo has given so much! And he's been so faithful.

Chorus1:   Shhh! He has something to say to us. Let's listen..

Rambo: My old and aged friends, listen to my words. Life is too short and the joys of life are few. I think you should live for today as best you can. Take heed and pass through every day and night with as much happiness as you can muster. I hope that every person I love is free of sadness and enjoys a life without sorrowful thoughts.

Chorus1:   Rambo is so kind!

Chorus2:   I love Rambo. He has always been a source of comfort.

Chorus1:   But he is so sad.

Chorus2:   Do you blame him?   Where is George Washington?   Putin Xi is going to burn George Washington's family alive and our friend has to stand by helplessly and watch.

Chorus1:   I would help but I'm too old.

Chorus2:   Me   too.   The   young   people   have abandoned George Washington.

Rambo: Old friends, remember time does not care about our hopes. He wrecks the little hope. Time flies and passes. Look at me. I am a man who made a mark amongst his fellows and achieved great fame. If you ask anyone, they'll tell you about how great I was and all the magnificent ways in which I won wars. But, let me tell you the sad truth about life. Fortune in a single day has robbed me of fame. I am like a feather that has been lifted up by wind and floats away toward the sky.   Wealth, fame, high reputation - none of these are fixed or will stay with you always.

Chorus1:   So sad!

Chorus2:   Rambo has lost his will to live!

Rambo: Farewell friends of my own age.   Look upon your friend for this is the last time you will see me alive.

End Episode 05

Episode 06: Introduction to George Washington

Chorus1:   Wait, who is walking this way?

Chorus2:   Can it be the person I think it is?

Chorus1:   It is!

Chorus2:   I can't believe it! He has returned!

G. Wash.: Hello, George Washington has returned! I say hello to my Internet, to electricity, and to all the technological advancements that make modern life possible. I feel such joy and happiness! Everyone, I, George Washington, traveled back in time and have returned with Andy Warhol who is going to make everyone famous for fifteen minutes.

Chorus1:   He's back!

Chorus2:   He'll save his family!

G. Wash.:   But, wait! Now that I have returned to my proper time, what is this sight that greets me? Why are my wife and sons dressed for a funeral? Why is my father weeping? Has something happened to my family while I was gone? Has fate sent me a wicked turn? Here comes my wife, she'll tell me what's going on.

Betsy Ross: George Washington, my husband! I am so happy you have returned to your family. You are the dearest of all mankind to me!

Rambo: You are a ray of light that has appeared to rescue your father! Is it really you? You have arrived just in time.

G. Wash.: Father, I don't understand why you are so sad and in dressed as though going to a funeral. I arrived home to find confusion.

Betsy Ross: Oh, husband! We are ruined and about to be killed. Forgive me, father-in-law for speaking first but I am in anguish. Husband, our children's lives have been threatened. We were about to be burnt alive.

G. Wash.: What a sad greeting for a returning hero! How did this happen?

Betsy Ross: First, my father is dead!

G. Wash.: What? How? Who dealt the fatal blow?

Betsy Ross: Putin Xi killed him and took over the city.

G. Wash.: How? In a fair fight or battle? Was the city suffering from affliction? Was the land sick and weak?

Betsy Ross: Yes, sick with faction and civil war. Now Putin Xi rules our city as its master.

G. Wash.:   When I arrived, why were you terrified and panicked?

Betsy Ross: Putin Xi has promised to burn your father, me, and our sons alive.

G. Wash.:   He wanted to kill my babies?

Betsy Ross: He was afraid they would avenge my father's death.

G. Wash.:   They're dressed as though they're heading to their own funeral.

Betsy Ross: They are! We were prepared to be burnt alive before you returned.

G. Wash.:   You were all going to die a violent terrible death. Where were our friends?

Betsy Ross: Husband, we have been deserted by every friend. As soon as word reached our city that you were dead we became bereft of friends.

G. Wash.:   Everyone thought I was dead? Why? How did such a bleak and desperate thought get in your heads?

Betsy Ross: Your cousin sent messengers saying your time travel failed.

G. Wash.: Really? Why aren't you living in our home?

Betsy Ross: We were forcibly removed! They tossed and dragged your father from his bed.

G. Wash.: No mercy or shame to treat an old man so poorly?.

Betsy Ross: Mercy or shame? Putin Xi doesn't know the goddess.

G. Wash.: Was I so poor in friends? Were they rare in my absence?

Betsy Ross: Who has friends during a time of misfortune?

G. Wash.: They forget my victories against the British?

Betsy Ross: Husband, I'll tell you again - misfortune has no friends.

End Episode 06

Episode 07: Putin Xi Prepares to Kill George Washington' Family

Chorus1: Oh! I can't wait for Putin Xi to get what's his. George Washington will get his revenge!

Chorus2: Now that George Washington is back, Putin Xi will be dealt with.

Chorus3: Shhh! I want to listen.

Putin Xi: Come on Rambo, it is time. Go back inside that house and bring Betsy Ross and those three boys out here. Tell them to come out here and prepare to die. I can't wait to smell your burning flesh. I have arranged for a big party to be held here so lots of people can watch you burn alive.

Rambo: Putin Xi, you are the ruler of this city but why do you take such pleasure in persecuting me? Why do you want me to suffer in misery? This zeal you show to murder my son's family is too much! It is over and above normal decency. You should be more moderate.

Chorus1:   Rambo speaks the truth.

Chorus2:   Yes, Putin Xi speaks with such disdain for human emotions and empathy. There is no reason for him to be happy about watching and smelling someone burn alive.

Chorus3:   Shhh! I want to listen.

Rambo: You are my lord and master. Lord or not, I ask you to temper your zeal. You say my son is dead and all I ask is you stop insulting me. Since my son is dead, you should act with more decency and let me grieve.

Chours1:   Good for Rambo!

Rambo: Since you are so eager to impose your death sentence on my grandchildren, we acquiesce and are prepared to do your will.

Putin Xi: Oh, really?   Well, then, where is Betsy Ross? Where are your grandchildren?

Rambo: Let's see? I believe, I guess, so far as I can make out, from outside, looking through this gate...

Putin Xi: Speak! What is she doing? Where is she ? Be specific.

Rambo: I see her sitting inside the house inside the room with her family's mementos.

Putin Xi: That makes sense. She's reliving all of her memories. I'm sure she's thinking I will take pity on her memories.

Rambo: No, she's calling her dead husband to return to this time.

Putin Xi: Ha! George Washington is lost in time. He's a husband who is nowhere seen or will ever be seen. He will never return to this city.

Rambo: Maybe he succeeded in traveling across time?

Putin Xi: Sure, right! Rambo, go inside the house and bring your daughter-in-law out here now. It is time for them to be burnt alive.

Rambo: If I do as you ask, I'll be complicit in her murder. Will you really make me an accomplice?

Putin Xi: If such scruples bother you then I will go inside on my own and drag the mother and her children outside. Time to put a painless ending to this troublesome affair!

Rambo: Walk along the path, Putin XI, and go meet your fate. Old and aged friends, Putin Xi enters George Washington's house at precisely the right time.

Chorus1:   This murderer marches fairly to his doom.

Chorus2:   George Washington's wrath is waiting for him. This villain thinks he will slay George Washington's family but George Washington will slay him instead!

Rambo: I am going inside to watch Putin Xi fall and die. The sight of a foe, an evil enemy, being slain and paying the full price for his deeds, gives me pleasure.

Chorus1:   Evil has changed sides and fortunes have turned. George Washington has returned from his travels across time!

Chorus2:   George Washington is alive! Hail justice!

Chorus1:   Hail retribution! Putin Xi enters the house and will be punished. Joy floods my eyes and makes tears burst forth.

Chorus2:   Retribution has been beyond my hopes and expectations!

End Episode 07

Episode 08: Sgt. Pepper Appears

Chorus1:   Old friends! Do you feel a shift in your mind?

Chorus2:   I feel as though my mind is revealing something scary and terrifying about myself.

Chorus1:   I want to run away!

Chorus2:   I do too! But, it is coming from inside me! I can't run from this.

Chorus1:   What is happening?

Sgt. Pepper: Do not be scared, old men. My name is Sgt. Pepper and I'm a psychological insight. I have not come to harm you, only to prepare you for what is about to happen.

Chorus1:   Are you saying something?

Chorus2:   I'm hearing voices!

Sgt. Pepper: I have been sent here by John Lennon. But, don't be afraid. John Lennon is not upset with any of you, only with George Washington. We have come to demolish him and his family. All of our war forces are marshaled against the house of one single man, George Washington.

Chorus1:   What is going on?

Chorus2:   I am hearing voices!

Sgt. Pepper: Now that George Washington has returned from his travels across time, John Lennon has decided it is time for him to be punished.

Chorus1:   I am so scared!

Chorus2:   Where is that voice coming from?

Sgt. Pepper: John Lennon has decided that George Washington will be burdened with the guilt of murdering his own children. Madness, come on down!

Chorus1: What is going on? Where did that wind come from?

Chorus2: My mind is so cloudy! I can't think straight. I hear voices and see visions.

Sgt. Pepper: Old men, my friend is going to enter George Washington's mind, drive him mad, and make him murder his family!

Chorus1: I'm so scared!

Chorus2: I'm shaking with fear!

Sgt. Pepper: Go ahead, darling. Enter into George Washington's psyche and create a child-murdering frenzy. Stir up and confound his mind. Make his feet twitch and shudder. Wind him up, shake out his sails, and set his sails of death up high. His own hands will murder his sons and then he will understand how angry John Lennon is with him. If this man escapes punishment, how can anyone understand the concept of time again?

End Episode 08

Episode 09: George Washington Murders His Family

Messenger: George Washington just killed Putin Xi!

Chorus1: Yea!

Chorus2: George Washington got his revenge!

Messenger: Now, George Wasington is gathering his family. They are pledging allegiance to the flag.

Chorus1: Exactly as they should.

Chorus2: George Washington is showing his children how to properly celebrate vanquishing an enemy.

Messenger: Wait! George Washington has stopped reciting the pledge of allegiance. He just stands there in silence.

Chorus1: Oh, no!

Messenger: The look on his face! His eyeballs are bloodshot and they roll wildly. His mouth oozes foam which covers his beard.

Chorus2:   What is happening?

Messenger: George Washington is laughing like a madman! He is saying something. I can't understand because he is speaking in a frenzy. Wait. He is saying, 'I won't finish this pledge of allegiance until I have also killed my cousin. Why should I say the pledge twice when once is enough!'

Chorus1:   Why is he talking about his cousin who sent him off to travel across time?

Chorus2:   That cursed cousin!

Messenger: Oh, no! George Washington has torn down the flag and poured imaginary lighter fluid on it.   Now, he's lighting an imaginary match and watching an imaginary flag burn.

Chorus1:   What?

Chorus2:   That voice we heard! It said it was going to make George Washington kill his children.

Messenger: Now, George Washington wants weapons. He's talking about getting on his boat and going across the Delaware. He wants to fight the British, set the colonies free, and set up a new country.

Chorus1:   What is George Washington talking about?

Chorus2:   He's inside his house! He has become delusional!

Messenger: He's talking about finding the British agents who taxed his property. He says he is going to Mt. Vernon to find his muskets.

Chorus1:   He's lost in his mind.

Chorus2:   What could possibly explain this? None of this makes sense?

Messenger: Oh, my! George Washington is acting as though he's rowing a boat. He's giving directions to imaginary people who row an imaginary boat.

Chorus1:   He's delusional!

Messenger: The people inside the house don't know what to do. Some of them look like they are going to laugh but others look terrified.

Chorus1:   Of course! He's acting mad and out of control.

Chorus2:   What explains his behavior?

Messenger: George Washington is chasing his children from room to room. He's stopped. Oh, no! George Washington shot his oldest son in the face!

Chorus1:   He killed his son!

Chorus2:   This is a tragedy!

Messenger: Betsy Ross is screaming at George Washington to stop. She's telling him she loves him and that his family loves him. Oh, no! George Washington murdered the infant in the most horrible way!

Chorus1:   George Washington killed his own infant!

Chorus2:   What could be worse than that!

Messenger: Now, George Washington is screaming terrible and fearful threats. Hold on. Rambo has grabbed George Washington and is yelling into his face. He's saying, 'Son, what are you doing? Why are you killing your children?'

Chorus1:   What does George Washington say?

Messenger: He pushed Rambo aside. Oh, no! George Washington shot Betsy Ross who stood in front of her last remaining child. Oh, no! George Washington has just shot his last son!

Chorus1:   What has happened?

Chorus2:   How could George Washington behave like this?

Messenger: Hold on a second. George Washington is looking around the house for Rambo. Oh, no! George Washington has aimed his gun at Rambo and is about to shoot!

Chorus1:   Will Rambo be saved?

Chorus2: Is George Washington going to kill his whole family?

End Episode 09

Episode 10: George Washington Realizes What He Has Done

G. Wash.: Why am I lying here tied to this column? Why has my house crashed down? What has happened to me?

Rambo: Son, are you sober or are you still in the grips of some murderous madness?

G. Wash.: I don't remember being mad!

Rambo: My son, look at the bodies. See your children's corpses.

G. Wash.: Oh, horror! What hideous sight is here? What sorrow is this?

Rambo: My son, against your sons you waged an unnatural war.

G. Wash.: War? What do you mean? Say who killed these children.

Rambo: You and your weapons, my son. You went into a murderous rampage and killed everyone you love.

G. Wash.: Father, what are you saying?

Rambo: My son, I am saying you went distraught and, in a fit of madness, killed your sons.

G. Wash.: Have I also murdered my wife?

Rambo: Yes. All this, George Washington, is the work of your own unaided hand.

G. Wash.: Woe is me. I'm wrapped in a cloud of sorrow and surrounded by sighs and groans.

Rambo: I lament and groan for the fate you suffer, my son

G. Wash.: Did I smash my house to pieces or incite others?

Rambo: I only know that your life is undone and you are ruined.

G. Wash.: Where was I when my frenzied madness seized me and destroyed my life?

Rambo: In the moment it seized you, you were surrounded by your family and reciting the pledge of allegiance.

G. Wash.: Oh, me! Why didn't I murder myself? How could I murder my sons without killing myself. I must commit suicide and I must do it now. Wait! Before I can put my plans to die into action, I have a new hurdle to jump. My friend Donald Trump is coming this way. I am so ashamed! I will veil my head in the darkness of my cloak to hide myself. If I allow my friend to see me, the experience will cause him pain.

End Episode 10

Episode 11: Introduction to Donald Trump

D. Trump: Rambo, old friend! I have arrived to help George Washington. I heard a rumor that Putin Xi usurped this city, became your enemy, and waged war against you. When I heard this, I came to help and repay my good friend.

Chorus1: That is what a good friend does.

Chorus2:   A friend helps another when they are in a time of need.

D. Trump: George Washington saved me when he went back in time and now I want to reciprocate.

Chorus1:   A good friend reciprocates.

Chorus2:   To be there and to reciprocate are signs of a good friend.

D. Trump: Why is the ground covered in corpses? Have I arrived too late? Wait! These are only boys! Boys are not sent to battle or war.   I must be discovering another type of disaster.

Rambo: Donald Trump, you've arrived from the new city.

D. Trump: Rambo! This is how you greet me after we haven't seen each other for such a long time?

Rambo: I have too much sadness to greet you any other way! The heavens have delivered and afflicted us with great suffering.

D. Trump: Whose children are these over which you weep and grieve?

Rambo: Donald Trump, these are my grandchildren, George Washington's own children! Oh, my unfortunate son! He was both their father and butcher. He had a hardened heart when he did the bloody deed.

D. Trump: What? You are saying George Washington killed his own family? How? Why? I don't understand.

Rambo: Oh, Donald Trump! George Washington was taken over by a wild fit of frenzied madness! Out of nowhere, he began chasing his sons around his house. He bashed them with his fists and shot them full of holes with his guns.

D. Trump: Oh, no! Rambo, please stop! This is a horrible story about George Washington. Please, tell me something better.

Rambo: Oh, how I wish I could do that, Donald Trump but I can't.

D. Trump: What dreadful things you say!

Rambo: Fortune has spread her wings and we are ruined.   The madness of George Washington has ruined everything. We are gone! This is our end!

D. Trump: I see John Lennon's work and carnage. Who is this man lying here among the corpses, old man?

Rambo: Donald Trump, that's my son. Oh, he's an enduring warrior.   A son of many miseries who marched on the British and started a new country.

D. Trump: Oh, woe for George Washington.   Was there ever a man who was caused to suffer so much?

Rambo: No, George Washington's madness is too much. Never will you find another person who chose to suffer for his country.

D. Trump: Tell me, why does he lie there and pretend to hide? Why does he veil his head with his cloak?

Rambo: He is ashamed! Your kindness and love make him ashamed to meet your eyes. His own shame is too great and he thinks it will cause you suffering.

D. Trump: Uncover his head. I have come to sympathize and share in his grief.

Rambo: Son, pull away that cover from your eyes. Let the sun see your face. It is a hard task to stand up against one's tears. My child, I know how angry you can become and I implore you not to use that anger against yourself. Restrain your savage lion's temper. You don't have to commit suicide. You can choose to live. Your anger at yourself causes you to rush forth across a path to create more bloodshed. Son, please! Don't be so eager to add one woe upon another.

End Episode 11

Episode 12: Donald Trump Defines True Friendship

Chorus1: Now that Donald Trump has arrived, maybe he can help George Washington.

Chorus2: I hope so. George Washington is so angry at himself for what he's done.

Chorus1: He keeps talking about suicide.

Chorus2: I know. He is so upset, he wants to kill himself!

D. Trump: Hey, you. Yes, you. Lying down there, huddled in the depths of your misery. I am calling you. Come and show your face to your friends. The darkest blackness wouldn't hide the pains of this catastrophe.

Chorus1: Good! Donald Trump doesn't let George Washington hide.

Chorus2: When a friend is in pain and suffering, a friend wants him to talk and share. That is the best way to show love and reciprocity.

Chorus1: Yes, the act of communication where you share your feelings and a friend is there to understand and help.

Chorus2: That is true friendship!

D. Trump: Hey, you! Stop moving your hands. Use your mouth. I don't speak in hand gestures. Are you trying to say something about murdering your family? Are you afraid that I will run away because of your horrible deeds? It doesn't matter to me, George Washington. I will suffer and share your fate.

Chorus1:   A true friend!

Chorus2:   George Washington is so lucky to have a true friend who has arrived to share his misfortune.

D. Trump: George Washington, whatever good fortune I have began with you and I hate a friend whose gratitude grows old. It is a terrible man who sails in a friend's happy moments but is unwilling to share the ship of poor fortune with him. George Washington, get up and uncover your poor face. Let me have a good look at you. Lift your eyes and look at me, you poor wretch. Come now, accept your horrible actions so that you may endure your life.

Chorus1:   Harsh words.

Chorus2: Yes, but they are true.

Chorus1: What other option does George Washington have?

Chorus2: His only recourse is to accept and endure.

Chorus1: Thankfully, Donald Trump has arrived to show what it means to be a good friend.

End Episode 12

Episode 13: George Washington Contemplates Suicide

G. Wash: Like no other man, I am afflicted with suffering misfortunes.

D. Trump: George Washington, your misfortunes stretch from the earth to the heavens.

G. Wash: And that's why I've resolved to prepare myself to die.

D. Trump: How would that help? Do you think anyone cares about such threats?

G. Wash: Life has been remorseless in its anger toward me. I don't care anymore. It is time to die.

D. Trump: Hold your tongue, George Washington. Your presumptuous words could bring you even more pain and suffering.

G. Wash: My ship has too much weight. All I carry are pains of sorrow. I don't have room for anything else. Woe is me!

D. Trump: So what are you going to do? Where is your fury drifting you? How far will your anger take you?

G. Wash: I will die! It is time for me to leave this world.

D. Trump: George   Washington,   your   words, language, and speech are the same as a common person.

G. Wash: So?   You don't know my grief!   I can't endure life any longer.

D. Trump: Are these the words of the much endured General George Washington?

G. Wash: Yes, in life and on the battlefield I have endured. But, this is too much! Endurance must come in moderation and have a limit.

D. Trump: Am I speaking with General George Washington? Aren't you the founder of a great country?

G. Wash: So what? It is time for me to die.

D. Trump: George Washington, why do you want to die such a perverse and mindless death?

G. Wash: Hear me and listen as I reason. I was born to American ideals, whatever American ideals might mean or if they even exist, and all that has happened is that John Lennon has been angry with me. It doesn't matter that I crossed the Delaware, defeated the British, and created a new country. John Lennon won't leave me be. All I've done my whole life is work to create a country and what is my thanks? My cousin told me to perform a task and I did! I went back in time and brought Andy Warhol here to make everyone famous for fifteen minutes! And my reward was going mad and killing my family. Oh, woe is me! I can't continue living after performing such terrible deeds. John Lennon succeeded! George Washington will kill himself and leave the earth. Oh, why has John Lennon always hated me? How could I have lived my life differently? What choices could I have made? Is there anything I could have done that would have prevented me from murdering my whole family? Oh, woe is me! What a terrible person I am! What a terrible thing I have done! I don't deserve to live! I must kill myself immediately!

D. Trump: Oh, my poor friend George Washington. You performed the terrible deeds but John Lennon is behind all of your suffering. Please, think carefully if this is your reason to die. Think about everything that's happened to you throughout your life. Haven't you met people who performed terrible actions through no fault of their own or who were compelled to do horrible deeds? Who doesn't suffer? Your life is no more cursed than any other person's. It is a horrible and terrible thing that has happened here but every person commits terrible deeds. Every person has been touched by misery. George Washington, what you have done is terrible like nothing else. But, you still deserve to live. This action was not caused by malice. Are you a person who judges yourself more harshly than how you judge others? This action was awful and terrible. You must obey the law and leave this city. Accompany me to my city and I will provide you with a home, and a portion of my wealth. The people in my city have given me gifts for helping them and I will share these with you. The people of my city will speak well of General George Washington. This is how I will show you that I am a true friend. I came to your city to help you in a time of need. I have found that you committed this atrocious deed but I will not turn my back on you. I am your friend and I see that you are in need of friends. George Washington, when we have good fortune we do not need friends. We need friends when times are difficult and a person thinks no one will come to their aid.   George Wasington, I am here for you. I am here to be your friend.

End Episode 13

Episode 14: George Washington Chooses to Live

G. Wash: Dear friend, though I'm still in misery I have had a thought. If I kill myself, people might think General George Washington is a coward. If a man cannot stand against misfortune, how can he stand against an enemy? I'll hold on to life! I will come with you to your city. I thank you profusely. I have tasted pain and have rejected none. I have shed no tears nor did I think I ever would. But now it seems I must be Fate's slave.   Old father, I am now both murderer and exile. Give my sons a proper burial, father. After the burial, stay in this city, father. It will not be easy, but strengthen your heart to share in my misery.

D. Trump: George Washington, my friend, it is time to stop crying. Come, let's leave!

G. Wash: I can't! My limbs are frozen.

D. Trump: I understand. Even powerful people like yourself are overpowered by misfortune.

G. Wash: I wish I could turn into a rock, because a rock doesn't have any memories and then I wouldn't have to remember all of my troubles.

D. Trump: Enough of this.   Give your hand to a helping friend.

G. Wash: Oh, D. Trump! Take care not to touch me. I don't want you to touch the murder blood that stains my clothes.

D. Trump: George Washington, leave it be. I am not concerned

G. Wash: Oh, Donald Trump! Now that I have lost my sons, I shall regard you as a son.

D. Trump: Come, put your arm around my neck and I'll lead the way.

G. Wash: A pair of friends, one of which is wretched in his misery. Old father, this is the sort of friendship a person ought to make. One that is reciprocal. Where a friend stands next to you no matter what you've done.

Rambo: Donald Trump comes from a good city.

G. Wash: Oh, turn me around so that I can see my sons once more.

D. Trump: Do you think it will work like some soothing drug?

G. Wash: I need to see them again. Oh father, I need to put my arms around you!

Rambo: Here I am with a loving embrace, my son. We both wish the same thing.

D. Trump: George Washington, have you forgotten all the battles you've won?

G. Wash: Why do you ask about my battles? Of course I haven't forgotten. But those didn't cause me grief.

D. Trump: You are speaking with too much emotion. This is not the way to win praise. If people see you acting like this they will say you behave without nobility.

G. Wash: You think I lack nobility? Those weren't your words a moment ago.

D. Trump: Well, George Washington, this grief and emotion is not noble behavior.   The George Washington of the olden days, the General George Washington who crossed the Delaware, defeated the British, and founded a country wouldn't be weeping and crying. He would be stoic and brave.

G. Wash: Donald Trump, when we were last in a precarious predicament how did you behave?

D. Trump: Even worse than you are now. In fact, I acted worse than any man who has ever lived. I was a coward. There is no one who would say that I acted

without courage.

G. Wash: Then how can you judge me?

D. Trump: Exactly! Let's go! My city awaits!

G. Wash: Farewell, old father!

Rambo: And to you too, my son!

G. Wash: Father, please bury my sons according to

the rituals.

Rambo: I will, my son. But what about me? Who

will bury me, my son?

G. Wash: I will, father.

Rambo: You will? When?

G. Wash: After your death, father.

Rambo: But how? You can't return to this city. You

have murdered your family and are now banished. I

don't understand.

G. Wash: Father, don't worry. I will bring you to the

new city but until then you have to bear this burden.

You need to bury my sons and live alone in this city

without a house or friends. And I, a person who has shamefully murdered his wife and sons, will follow Donald Trump to his new city where I will be treated well. I say to everyone who will listen, it is better to have a good friend than wealth or power.

Chorus1: Let us leave this place full of tears and sadness.

Chorus2: We have lost our best friends.

Exit all

End of Madness "Washington"